Littlenose

1J

More adventures of

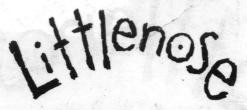

Littlenose the Hero

Littlenose the Hunter

Littlenose the Joker

Littlenose the Explorer

Littlenose
the Leader

JOHN GRANT

ILLUSTRATIONS by ROSS COLLINS

SIMON AND SCHUSTER

SIMON AND SCHUSTER

Littlenose to the Rescue was first published in 1975
Littlenose the Leader and The Music Stick
were first published in 1977
The other stories were first published in 1982
in Great Britain by The British Broadcasting Corporation

This collection published by Simon and Schuster UK Ltd, 2008
A CBS COMPANY

Text Copyright © John Grant 1975, 1977, 1982 and 2008
Illustrations copyright © Ross Collins, 2008

3 5 7 9 10 8 6 4 2

Simon & Schuster UK Ltd
1st Floor
222 Gray's Inn Road
London WC1X 8HB

A CIP catalogue record for this book is available from the British Library

ISBN: 978-1-84738-200-9

Typeset by Ana Molina
Printed and bound in Great Britain by Cox & Wyman Ltd, Reading, Berkshire

Contents

Littlenose the Leader

A Neanderthal man who wanted meat to
feed his family had to go out and hunt for
it. This was no easy job because the
animals had to be tracked and stalked. The
hunters knew where to lie in wait, since
most animals were to be found in the same
places at the same times of the year. But
from time to time the system went wrong,
as it did once for Littlenose's tribe.

The Old Man called a meeting one day. "As we all know," he said, "the supply of game has been very poor, and if we are to get through the winter we must find out how the game herds are moving. A reconnaissance party will leave at dawn."

Littlenose was very excited. As an apprentice hunter he would accompany the party. Dad wasn't excited. He thought that taking Littlenose was just asking for trouble! Littlenose spent the evening

packing his hunting equipment – his flint knife, fire-lighting flints and a spare pair of furs. He was about to put in one of his special treasures when Dad said: "What on earth do you want with that?"

It was a piece of flat bone carved with a picture of hunters attacking a giant fish. It had been given to Littlenose by Urk, a strange little man who had stayed with them once. "I like it and it might bring me luck!" said Littlenose.

"It's an extra weight to carry," said Dad.

In the cold darkness the reconnaissance party set off next morning. Nosey, the Chief Tracker, led the way, and by nightfall they were far from home. But they had found no game herds.

"Early days yet," said Nosey confidently.

And so they went on. They were in completely strange country, but they had great faith in Nosey, who led them in a long line, his handsome nose pointing to the ground and snuffling in a very expert way from time to time. Littlenose trudged along cheerfully enough. Urk's carved bone was safely hidden inside his furs. He was sure it was lucky.

Certainly, the reconnaissance party wasn't lucky. They found enough small game for themselves, but nothing of any size. Nosey had stopped saying "Early days", and one mid-day they held a conference. They came to two decisions. One: it was time to return home, and two: they were lost.

For almost a month they had followed Nosey without bothering about where they were going. They asked Nosey if he had any idea where they might be, but he just shrugged and said, "Search me!"

It was several days since they had seen any trees, and the sky had a permanently grey, snowy look to it. Each day was colder than the last, and the nights were getting longer. But sitting down talking wasn't going to help, so they chose a likely-looking direction and set off for what they hoped was home. And to make matters worse, snow began to fall.

At nightfall, they wrapped themselves in their hunting robes and dreamed of warm caves and dry furs. For six nights they did this. The snow didn't stop until late on the seventh day, when it was growing dusk. They saw the last of the sun disappearing over the horizon, and bare, rocky hills ahead. Just before darkness, the hunters found a cave where they prepared to spend a cold and dry, but hungry, night. For by now all their provisions were gone, and there had been no animals to hunt during the days of snow.

Next morning Littlenose was first awake, and he ran out of the cave to see what there was to see. It wasn't much. The ground sloped steeply down, then levelled out to a flat plain which disappeared into the mist. There were patches of gravel, otherwise,

the land lay under a blanket of snow as
far as the eye could see. Littlenose saw
something moving in the distance,
something large and dark that crawled
rapidly along the ground before vanishing
abruptly. He rubbed his eyes, but the
creature had gone. However, at the foot of
the slope, he found some wood. At least
they would have a fire.

Warm at last, but still hungry, the
hunters decided that their first task was to
find some food. They only half believed
Littlenose's story of the animal he had seen,
but it was all they had to go on.

Accordingly, they set off down the slope
and across the snow field. It wasn't as
smooth as it looked at a distance, and there
were many ridges and hollows.

As they reached the top of a ridge

Littlenose cried out in excitement: "There it is!" And they saw the most curious sight. A large, fat animal was slithering along, apparently without any legs. With a cry, the men raced towards it, but before they had taken more than a few steps it suddenly flipped its rear end in the air and vanished.

"It's gone down its burrow," cried Littlenose, and sure enough there was a large hole at the spot. But it wasn't a burrow. They reached the circular hole and found themselves looking into a pool of water. Nosey reached down with his spear. "It's bottomless," he said. He put his fingers to his lips. "It's salt," he said. "We must be close to the sea."

As he spoke, the last of the mist rolled away and they saw a dark blue sea just a short distance from where they stood.

"We can catch fish," said Dad, and started walking towards the shore.

This time it was Dad who shouted: "Quick! Don't let it get away!" Another of the odd animals rolled over and began humping and slithering its way towards the sea. They watched it in disappointment as it slithered with barely a ripple into the water. From the water's edge the hunters watched their lost prey surface and look back at them. Then they saw something else. Moving at incredible speed through the water, was a tall, pointed black object. The object rose higher in the water and now they saw that it was a fin on the biggest fish they had ever seen! In a shower of spray, a pair of gaping jaws filled with gleaming teeth bore down on the swimming animal. Then it was gone, and a huge black and white fish shape was slipping back into the green depths. No one spoke, until Nosey cried, "RUN FOR YOUR LIVES!"

A second black and white monster was racing in a cloud of spray, half out of the water, and straight towards the Neanderthal hunters. They turned to watch, and to their horror the fish didn't even slow down as it neared the water's edge. It reared high in the air and crashed down on the snow . . . and the ground split apart beneath! But it wasn't ground. It was ice! They were standing on the frozen sea, which was breaking up in cracks and fissures as the fish made another attempt to get at them. The ice bucked and heaved as they fled for the distant beach.

Once they had got their breath back and had stopped shaking, the hunters decided

to return to the cave and discuss their next
move. They were within a few paces of the
cave when without warning they found
themselves surrounded by a crowd of fur-clad
figures. They looked roughly Neanderthal,
but their noses were flat, their eyes slanting,
and their hair hung in fringes on their

foreheads. Their leader made unmistakeable signs, and the hunters dropped their spears and raised their hands. Their captors ran their hands expertly over their furs and took away their flint knives. When they came to Littlenose, however, one man took his knife, then paused as he found the carved bone under his furs. Then he shouted a command, and his men marched the prisoners at spear point away from the cave and along the shore.

Famished as well as exhausted from their adventure, Littlenose's party felt they had been marching for ever when they came round a headland and saw a large crowd waiting. Men, women and children crowded about them, pulling and pushing and crying out in a strange language. There were caves at the foot of a cliff, and the Neanderthal hunters were led into one of them, while a man with a spear stood guard outside.

"What's going to happen to us?" asked Littlenose. Before anyone could answer a man appeared and beckoned to Littlenose. "Who, me?" asked Littlenose in a startled voice. The man nodded and pointed. With an attempt at a brave grin, Littlenose followed him out of the cave. The man seemed quite friendly, and took Littlenose's hand over some of the rockier patches until they reached a large fire.

Around the fire were sitting some very important-looking men, one of whom seemed to be the leader. He waved Littlenose towards him and said something in a kindly voice. Littlenose said, "Yes sir," and smiled. And all the people round about cheered

and clapped. The leader now squatted
down by the fire, while everyone gathered
around. Then with a stick he began to
draw in the sand, all the time talking in his
strange language. Slowly, Littlenose began
to understand. He recognised some of the
words he had learned from Urk, the stranger

who had made his carved bone ornament.
The leader told about his tribe and their
life by the shores of the frozen sea. He
described the animals they hunted. The
slithering creature on the ice he called a
seal. Seals made very good eating and
provided furs for clothing. The biggest
creature, however, was the whale. Here he
laid Littlenose's bone carving on the
ground and proceeded to draw a bigger
version of it. It was like an enormous fish,
bigger than ten mammoths, and was only
caught in very exceptional circumstances
like being stranded in shallow water at low
tide. He looked enquiringly at Littlenose.
Had they seen any whales, he asked?

Littlenose thought, then with his finger
he drew in the sand as well as he could the
hunters' narrow escape.

The people looked at each other in amazement, while the chief shook his head and said, "Phew!" It appeared that they had escaped from the deadly killer whale, which attacked everything and was afraid of nothing.

The leader signalled Littlenose to stand beside him. Then he said something to the crowd and hung the carved bone around Littlenose's neck once more. He gave him back his spear and flint knife while everyone cheered. By signs, the leader told Littlenose that he was to go back to the cave and fetch the others.

At the cave the hunters crowded round. "How did you escape? How did you get away?" they asked.

"Listen very carefully," said Littlenose. "You must do exactly as I tell you."

"What?" spluttered Dad.

"The Snow People
(that's what they call
themselves) think that I
am your leader," said
Littlenose. "And that is
my badge of office." He
fingered the carved bone.

"Well I'll– " began
Dad, but Littlenose,
beginning to enjoy himself, said sternly,
"You'll do as you're told. Or be left behind.
They're preparing a feast. In MY honour."

That changed everything. Everyone
became cheerful, except Dad, who gave
Littlenose a very wait-till-I-get-you-home
look. Littlenose was enjoying himself even
more as he bustled about shouting "Come
on now! Smarten yourselves up! Straighten

those furs there!" Then he led the hunters
out to meet the Snow People. The feast
seemed a long time in coming, but when it
did, it was beyond their wildest dreams.
Afterwards they sat back and watched a
display of dancing and music which first
excited them, then began to lull them to

sleep. It was all they could do to make
their way back to the cave.

They had barely closed their eyes, it
seemed, before they were wakened by loud
shouts. They rushed outside. It was growing
light, and Snow People were dashing about
shouting: "WHALE! WHALE!"

"Come on," cried Littlenose, and the
Neanderthal hunters joined the crowd
streaming along the shore. They went
round the rocky headland and saw a broad
bay. Ice clung to the shores, and great
floating fragments cut it off from the open
sea. The crowd spread round the shores of
the bay, and Littlenose could see no whale.
Then the water erupted in a giant cloud of
spray, and Littlenose almost turned and ran
as something black, shining, and bigger
than TWENTY mammoths rose out of the

water, blowing clouds of steaming breath
into the icy air and beating the water with
a giant tail.

The Snow People shouted and began
running across the shore and onto the
floating pieces of ice. Long spears were
thrown, and the whale dived again. But
when it surfaced it was closer to the shore.
Each time it came up the Snow People

drove it further in until with a great lashing of its tail it stopped. It had grounded in the shallows. In a moment the hunters were all over it, and in no time at all, it seemed, the dead whale was being cut up and carried back to the caves.

There was another celebration party that night, and Littlenose was guest of honour. The Snow People were quite sure that it

was he who had brought them luck.

They left for home the next day, with directions and plenty of provisions from their hosts. They were each given a commemorative carved bone. Littlenose was given one slightly larger than the others, as became a leader.

Littlenose's leadership lasted until they were out of sight of the Snow People's caves. Then Dad said, "Enough's enough. Now, tuck that thing back inside your furs again and keep your eyes peeled for firewood."

When they reached home, many weeks later, Littlenose had almost forgotten that for a short time he had been a leader. And he didn't really care. It was nice to look back on, but much more fun just being a Neanderthal boy.

Littlenose the Lifesaver

Despite its name, the weather during the
Ice Age was not just a matter of ice and
snow. It rained a lot, more than in the
Good Old Days according to the older
Neanderthal folk; but, the wind . . . that
was something else. The Neanderthal folk
lived in caves, which have no doors, so the
only protection against cold winds was to
get as far into the cave as possible, wear

every piece of fur they owned, and huddle over the fire, if the ferocious draughts hadn't blown it out.

However, wind wasn't entirely a bad thing. The fires which warmed the caves and cooked the food also kept wild animals at bay. So, the gathering of fuel was an important part of Neanderthal life. Most of the time it meant trudging off into the woods with a flint axe and laboriously dragging back fallen branches or even more laboriously cutting down a not-too-big tree.

But, in the autumn, as the last of the leaves were turning red, there would come a wind fit, you might think, to blow everything off the face of the earth. It didn't, but it blew down a great supply of limbs and branches, and even whole trees. The people would huddle in their caves and listen to the howling of the wind outside. "Ah," they would say wisely to one another, "it's an ill wind that doesn't blow *some* good!"

One morning, after a night of screaming gales, Littlenose set off with his dad and other men of the tribe to gather firewood. Although the wind had died somewhat with the coming of daylight, it was still blowing in strong gusts, and the wood-gatherers bent their heads into it as it tugged at their furs and tried to sweep them off their feet.

But the gale had done a good job. The

ground was strewn with enough fuel to last the whole tribe for a long time to come. The party made several trips back to the caves until there was nothing left worth gathering. Littlenose was weary from the work, and he hoped that now they could go home. Then Dad pointed to a patch of forest close to the river and much farther from home. "Let's try there," he shouted. "There's plenty of daylight left, and we can't have too much fire wood!" The others nodded, more or less enthusiastically, and off they trudged across the open plain towards the distant trees. Out of the shelter of the forest the wind pushed them this way and that, completely taking away Littlenose's breath. Half-way there he stopped. "Just give me a moment to get my breath back," he panted.

"Good idea," said one of the men. And they sat on the ground with their backs to the wind, which actually seemed to be less strong. In fact, when they stood up to go on their way they could have sworn that it was beginning to die away altogether.

The trees were still some way off when Littlenose pointed. "Look," he said, "we needn't go so far. There are lots of branches blown from the forest and lying about in the grass. Why not gather those?" Why not, indeed, the men agreed, and they scattered in all directions, picking up tree branches and piling them in handy piles for carrying home. And the wind was getting less, and a sort of eerie calm had fallen over the plain. The party were now well separated from one another, and Littlenose was working his way along the steep river bank when he heard a shout. One man was standing waving his arms and shouting. It sounded like a warning. Was it a woolly rhinoceros or a sabre-toothed tiger? He was pointing to the sky where a great black cloud had formed against the grey. "He must think it's going to rain," said Littlenose to himself. "What a fuss to make about a spot of rain!" Yet it didn't look like a rain cloud. It was low in the sky, with what looked like a long tail trailing towards the ground. The man shouted again. Something that sounded like "WHIRLWIND!"

"WHIRL . . . *what*?" thought Littlenose. Next moment he staggered as a gust of wind nearly bowled him over. There came another, and another, then a roaring in the air that grew louder every moment. The

men were by now running in all directions
as the strange black cloud rushed down
upon them. And Littlenose froze with horror
at what he saw. The tail of the cloud was a
swiftly spiralling column of wind which
sucked up branches, bushes, and even small

trees as it advanced over the plain.

Littlenose watched a clump of silver birches suddenly stripped of their leaves, and all but the biggest torn from the ground and carried high into the air, to be scattered moments later, smashed and broken on the flattened grass. Almost too late Littlenose began to run. He ran towards the river, while the whirlwind raced behind him, deafening him with its howl, and tugging roughly at his furs. At the last moment he saw a jumble of rocks and dived head first into a deep crevice.

It was like the end of the world. The whirlwind seemed to be trying to drag Littlenose out of his refuge while it showered him with leaves, branches, dirt and small stones.

Then it had gone; and Littlenose poked

his head out from the rocks and watched the whirlwind cross the river in a cloud of mud and water before twisting its way towards the distant hills.

Littlenose climbed up on to the river bank, stood up and looked all around.

And saw no one. The wind still blew in occasional strong gusts, and the path of the whirlwind was marked by a wide track of smashed and flattened trees and bushes, as if a huge herd of bison had stampeded. There was no sign of the men. He was alone. He ran out into the plain, and towards the forest. Everyone was gone! Swept away by the whirlwind? It was too awful to even think about. "Probably ran off home," thought Littlenose. "I'd better do the same." But he had only gone a couple of steps when he heard a noise. A human noise.

Someone had groaned. He ran back to the river bank, and there by the water's edge lay a figure. It was a man, lying face downward on a tangle of tree branches floating close to the edge. Littlenose waded in and started to drag the man towards the bank. He pulled him onto the shingle and rolled him onto his back. At least he was still breathing . . . but it wasn't the state of health that caught Littlenose's attention. He had thought that it might be one of the wood gatherers . . . but, far from it. The man who lay at his feet fluttering his eye-lids and spitting out water and bits of leaf was a STRAIGHTNOSE! A deadly enemy of the Neanderthal folk. He was tall and slim, with a slender neck and the straight, narrow nose that gave his people their name. Littlenose had one thought. *Run!*

By now the Straightnose had opened his eyes. He sat up, grabbed hold of Littlenose's wrist, and said something in his own language. Hoping for the best, Littlenose smiled as best he could, nodded, and said, "Yes, sir!"

The man frowned, then slowly got to his feet, still holding Littlenose. He seemed to have hurt his leg, and after a few stumbling steps he leaned on Littlenose for support. They made their way up the bank and on to the level plain. Littlenose started to say, "Well, time I was getting home . . ." The Straightnose didn't even pause to listen. Taking an even firmer grip of Littlenose's wrist and leaning even more heavily on his shoulder, he began to limp away from the river and, worse, away from home.

The river was far behind them when at

last they stopped. The man let go of
Littlenose, who was too weary to even
think of trying to run away. In any case he
had lost all sense of direction and had no
idea where he was. They had stopped by a
clump of bushes, and the Straightnose
reached under them and drew out a long,
dangerous-looking spear. He also drew out
a skin pouch with fruit and dried meat in
it. He handed some to Littlenose and they
sat on the ground to eat.

Littlenose wished the man would stop
staring. He pointed at Littlenose's berry-
sized nose, touched his own, and said
something in his own language. Again,
Littlenose hopefully replied, "Yes, sir!" and
smiled. He thought the man smiled slightly,
too, and kept on staring at him until he
suddenly pulled himself to his feet, and

Littlenose with him. When next he spoke,
Littlenose knew exactly what he meant,
and he picked up the food pouch and heaved
it on to his shoulder. The Straighnose no
longer held his wrist, but made Littlenose
walk in front while he leaned on his spear
for support instead of Littlenose's shoulder.

The sun was well down in the sky when
they next stopped to rest. The Straightnose
man's pace had been getting steadily slower,

which suited Littlenose, as the food pouch seemed to be getting steadily heavier. The Straightnose pointed in the direction of the setting sun and said something, then laid down the spear and stretched out on the grass for a nap, indicating by gestures that he thought Littlenose should do the same. Littlenose didn't lie down, but sat with his back to a handy tree stump and wondered if he would ever see home again. Perhaps he should get some sleep. His head nodded as he watched swaying grass heads against the sunset. Was something wrong? Grass heads swayed in the wind, but since the whirlwind there had not been a breath of wind. He stood up and peered into the growing dusk. The grass was still for a moment, then it swayed and parted as, barely twenty paces away, a large, hungry-looking hyena stepped into a clear patch.

Littlenose gasped and jumped back in fright, falling over the Straightnose's injured leg. The man grabbed him and shouted as he sat up. He shouted again, and had started to shake Littlenose when the hyena gave a low, chuckling cry, partly in surprise at the sound of a human voice, and partly in anticipation of a good evening meal. The man pushed Littlenose to one side and picked up his spear and, with only a moment's aim, threw it at the hyena. But, his bad leg gave way as he threw, and the spear flew over the animal's head and stuck in the ground. There was nothing left to do but run, and Littlenose did just that. Then he stopped, and looked back. The Straightnose was trying to follow him, but could only manage to hobble slowly, while the hyena steadily advanced, shoulders hunched, teeth gleaming, and giggling in its own unpleasant hyena way.

This could be Littlenose's chance. He could escape while his captor was busy with the hyena. That is, while the Straightnose was being eaten. Yet people only survived in the Ice Age by banding together to protect each other, and even Straightnoses were people!

Without another thought, Littlenose turned. He had no plan, but he had not saved the man from drowning just to feed a hungry hyena! The hyena had forgotten Littlenose, and now it was crouched, winding up for the final rush at his victim. It took one step . . . and yelped as a large stone hit it on the ear. It looked round and another stone bounced off its nose,

followed by one in the eye. This was unfair! Hyenas preyed on old, sick or injured victims, and here was an injured victim ripe for preying on. There was nothing in hyena rules about non-injured victims who threw stones! Whimpering, it pawed its bloody nose, and as another stone smacked it in the ribs it turned and loped off swiftly into the gathering night.

Littlenose walked back to the man, who held out his hand before retrieving the spear and signalling Littlenose to follow him with his food pouch. Their resumed march didn't last long. A bright glow appeared in the sky, and from the top of a ridge Littlenose found himself looking down on a large Straightnose encampment.

It was just as he had feared. He was going to be paraded as a prisoner . . .

and more than likely eaten if half the stories about Straightnoses were true! He had fallen into Straightnose hands once before, and had been extremely lucky to have escaped.

As they passed between the tents, a crowd of curious Straightnoses followed. Some Straightnose boys shouted at Littlenose, and one prodded him with a stick, but they backed off when his captor waved his spear and shouted back in their own language. A few more steps and they stood beside a fire while the whole Straightnose tribe gathered in a circle. Then the circle parted and a splendid figure approached, and beckoned to Littlenose.

It was the Chief, dressed in a long white fur cloak and with feathers in his hair. He said something to Littlenose, who didn't

understand, then turned to
the man who had brought
Littlenose.

And the man began
to relate his adventure.
He didn't just speak,
but mimed and
gestured and even
broke into a dance at
one point, so that
Littlenose found that
he could follow the
story quite well. The
man told how he had been out looking for
game when he spotted the Neanderthal
wood-gathering party. He had climbed a
tree to have a better look when the
whirlwind came and carried him with the
branches he was clinging to into the river.

He knew no more until Littlenose had pulled him out and helped him to walk and carry his equipment. And then (the man paused for dramatic effect), and then they had been attacked by the most ferocious hyena you could imagine – and this fearless Neanderthal boy had driven it off! At this the crowd went mad, clapping, shouting, cheering, until the Chief held up his hand.

There followed a long discussion between the Chief and the Straightnose men, no doubt about what was to be done with Littlenose. Not eaten, that was certain. The Chief had been looking closely at Littlenose for some moments, and when next he spoke, Littlenose was sure he caught the word "Redhead". Yes, there it was again. Boldly, Littlenose spoke up, "I have an Uncle Redhead. He has many

Straightnose friends." At the mention of Uncle Redhead, the Chief and his men smiled, the rest of the people laughed . . . and one pretty Straightnose girl blushed. After that, everything seemed to happen at once. Food and drink were produced, and people came up and spoke to Littlenose as he ate. Everyone seemed to want to talk about Uncle Redhead, although what they said Littlenose hadn't the faintest idea. The pretty girl showed him a picture of a beaver drawn on birch bark just like the one Uncle Redhead had made for Littlenose.

Then it was time to go. Littlenose was lifted on to the shoulders of a Straightnose hunter, and other hunters gathered around him. Everyone said a Straightnose "goodbye" while they shook his hand or patted his head. The pretty girl blew a kiss and said, "Redhead!" before disappearing into the crowd. The last goodbyes were said, and Littlenose was on his way home. The Straightnoses ran like the wind, taking it in turns to carry Littlenose, and just as dawn was breaking they came to the place where Littlenose had last seen his own people before the whirlwind came. The Straightnoses put him on the ground, shook his hand again, and were gone.

"What an adventure!" he thought. "Just wait until I tell them what nice people the Straightnoses really are. Not in the least

evil monsters that eat Neanderthal children."
Then he paused. Who was going to believe
him? Certainly not Dad. Nothing would
ever shake his fixed Neanderthal ideas
about the Straightnoses – and everything
else for that matter.

Ah, but what about Uncle Redhead? He
would believe him all right . . . particularly
the bit about the pretty Straightnose girl.

He'd tell the others that he had been
blown away by the whirlwind over the hills
and far away, and had been all night
walking home. All he wanted to do now
was to reach the family cave as quickly as
possible and curl up in bed in his own
special corner.

Littlenose the Marksman

Neanderthal men had to be good spear throwers. Accurate spear throwing could mean the difference between supper for a hunter's family – or supper for someone else's, like a sabre-toothed tiger's. Because of this, most hunters were very good at throwing spears, and some were brilliant. Dad was one of these (as he never stopped telling Littlenose), and he felt that it was a terrible disgrace that Littlenose was probably the worst spear thrower who had ever lived.

Littlenose's spear throwing might have been a joke, if it hadn't been so dangerous. All he had to do was appear at the entrance to the family cave carrying his boy-size spear, and the members of the tribe vanished like rabbits. It wasn't that Littlenose didn't practise. He went to lessons with the other Neanderthal boys, and practised each night while Dad shouted encouragement . . . and a lot of other things. But he still couldn't throw a spear properly.

One night, just as they were finishing supper, Dad said, "I've made up my mind. We're going to end this spear nonsense once and for all. Tomorrow I am taking you out to practise, and we are not coming home until you can get it right. In fact, we will start now, before you go to bed."

So, while Mum cleared up the supper things, Dad fetched his spear and gave Littlenose a lecture on the finer points of the art. Not that Littlenose needed the lecture; he could have given it himself, so many times had he heard it.

"The weight goes on the right foot," began Dad. "Shoulders square. Spear gripped firmly but lightly. Think of it as part of your arm. Eye on target. Smooth swing and follow-through."

And Littlenose did all of these things without, of course, actually letting go of the spear.

Dad beamed. "Lovely, lovely!" he cried. "What a beautiful action! You're taking after me at last. Do that tomorrow, and you'll be junior champion of the tribe."

Littlenose shrugged his shoulders. What a waste of time, spending tomorrow chucking a rotten old spear about when he could be having fun with Two-Eyes. However, he carried on practising until bedtime, and fell asleep sure that his arm was going to fall off.

Next morning, after breakfast, Dad got ready for Littlenose's lesson. Littlenose picked up the spear and stood near the cave entrance to wait. Might as well try a few loosening-up exercises, he thought. He held the spear firmly but lightly, weight on his right foot, and went through the smooth swing and follow-through action. And he forgot to hold onto the spear. It sailed out of the cave and straight through a pair of best furs hung out to dry by a neighbour. Naturally there was some unpleasantness, ending with the neighbour shouting, ". . . and take that boy of yours as far away as you can. And if you never bring him back it will be too soon!"

"That's another fine mess you've got me into," grumbled Dad, as they went into the forest. They walked a long way, until they came to a clearing, at the edge of which stood a tall tree. During the winter gales a big branch had broken off and left a scar on the trunk. The scar formed a circle with

rings, and Dad pointed at it. "That," he
explained, "is your target." He walked to
the opposite edge of the clearing and
scored a mark on the ground with his
spear. "Stand here," he said, "and try to
stick the spear in the centre of the circle.
Like this." And without even taking
particular aim, or so it seemed to
Littlenose, he threw the spear so that it
stuck, quivering, right in the centre of the
target. "Now you try," said Dad.

Littlenose held the spear firmly but lightly, and threw the spear exactly as he had practised the evening before. The spear whizzed through the air . . . and stuck in the tree about three hand widths above the target.

"A bit high," said Dad. "Try again." This time the spear stuck in about three hand widths *below* the target.

"Now," said Dad, "right in the middle this time." The spear hit a branch off to the left. Then to the right. Then down to the left. And up to the right. *Everywhere* but on the target.

And so it went on. When the sun was high in the sky, Dad was almost weeping with vexation, and the only mark on the target was the spot where Dad had hit it. All around, however, was peppered with spear-holes from Littlenose's unsuccessful efforts.

Dad looked at the sun. It was almost midday. "Have one more go," he said, wearily. "Then we'll go home for lunch. Let's see if we can tell Mum that at least you hit the *target* once, if not actually in the middle."

Littlenose sighed, gripped the spear in the correct manner, kept his eye on the target – and missed the tree altogether.

Dad jumped up and down. "I don't believe it," he cried. "How could any son of mine be so stupid? Go and fetch the spear, and we'll go home." For the first time that day, Littlenose began to feel faintly cheerful. He trotted round the tree and behind the bushes which grew at its foot. But there was no spear. "I can't find it," he called.

Dad joined him. "It must be somewhere," he said, impatiently. "You just haven't *looked* properly." But, he couldn't find it either. Dad and Littlenose poked about among the bushes and in the long grass . . . but no, spear.

"We might as well just go home," said Littlenose. "It's only an old spear."

"What do you mean? Old spear?" shouted Dad. "It was one of my best! And he began rummaging about among the bushes again. Littlenose had already lost what little interest he had in the problem of the lost spear and had wandered away a short distance. Suddenly he stopped, and called, "I think I know where it went. I think it's in *there*." And he pointed to a hollow tree trunk lying half-hidden in the long grass.

"Well, don't just stand there," said Dad. "Get it out."

Littlenose made a face. "You don't think I'm crawling in there?" he exclaimed. "It's dark and damp and smelly, and I bet it's full of spiders and earwigs and creepy-crawlies that go in your hair and inside your furs."

Dad gave him a look. "Hmph!" he said. "I suppose I'll have to get it myself, like everything else in this family." He got down

on all fours and began to grope his way
inside the hollow trunk. It was a tight
squeeze, and Littlenose watched as Dad's
head, then his shoulders, then the rest of
his body vanished from sight. He stood
scuffling his feet in the long grass, and
Dad's knees were just disappearing when
he kicked something hard. He bent down.
"Dad," he called, "I've found the spear!
You can come out."

And Dad's voice, sounding rather odd,
echoed from inside the tree: "I CAN'T!
I'M STUCK!"

Littlenose looked in amazement. All that

could be seen of Dad were his feet sticking out of one end of the log. "Can't you get out at all?" said Littlenose.

The noise that came from the log made Littlenose jump back. "In that case," he said, "I'd better get you out." He gripped Dad's ankles, leaned back, and heaved.

"STOP! STOP!" screamed Dad. "You're pulling my ears off!"

Littlenose let go, and walked round to the other end of the hollow log. "I'll try pushing," he said. "That ought to work." He sat down with his legs inside the tree and his feet against the top of Dad's head. Then he took a firm hold of the tree and pushed. "STOP!" yelled Dad again. "You're taking my nose off!"

"Well, there's nothing for it," said Littlenose. "I'll have to get help. Perhaps if

Mum boiled up some bear grease and poured it . . ."

But Dad interrupted in a panic-stricken voice: "You can't leave me like this," he cried. "I'm helpless. Anything might come along and bite me!"

"There might be a way," said Littlenose, thoughtfully. "If I pushed a bit, and pulled a bit, and used the spear as a lever, and you sort of kicked your feet . . . do you think you might be able to stand up?"

It took much more pulling, pushing, levering and kicking than Littlenose had imagined, but at length Dad managed to lurch unsteadily to his feet. And Littlenose burst out laughing.

"What's so funny?" said Dad hollowly through a narrow crack in the trunk.

"Nothing, really," said Littlenose, trying

to keep his face straight. "It's just that I've never seen a tree with feet before."

"Well, stop messing about, and get me home," said Dad.

"Right," said Littlenose. "Follow me." And he strode off in the direction of the caves.

Dad tottered for a few steps, banged into a tree and wandered around in a circle before he called: "I can't follow you! I can hardly see a thing through the crack."

"Oh, all right," said Littlenose patiently, "take my hand."

"How can I take your hand?" said Dad. "My arms are stuck inside this thing with me!"

"Don't worry," said Littlenose. "I'll take your branch."

"You'll what?" said a mystified Dad.

Littlenose didn't bother to try to explain.
He reached up and
got hold of a
branch still
attached to the
dead tree and
began to lead Dad
in the direction of
home, where he
was sure Mum
would know how to
get Dad out, probably, he still thought, by
using boiling bear fat.

They made good progress, with only the
occasional yell from Dad as Littlenose
accidentally led him through a patch of
nettles or over a sharp stone. Then Littlenose
was suddenly almost jerked off his feet as
Dad came to an abrupt halt. The dead tree

swayed about, while a wheezy voice panted through the crack: "I – can't – go – another – step! I'm – exhausted! It isn't – every – day – that – I – carry – trees – around – the – forest – like – this!"

"We're almost there," said Littlenose, encouragingly.

"You – go – on – and – fetch – Mum –" gasped Dad. "I'll – wait – here."

"Not here, you can't," said Littlenose. "You're right in the middle of the path! People won't be able to get past. I'll guide you to one side." He took Dad's branch again and moved him to one side. "He makes quite a handsome tree," thought Littlenose, as he looked back before running as fast as he could to fetch Mum.

As Littlenose's footsteps faded into the distance, Dad began to get his breath back.

He found that if he bent his knees the trunk took its own weight against the ground and he could rest. It wasn't too uncomfortable, and he began to relax, closed his eyes, and fell asleep.

Dad woke with the sound of voices. He twisted round and managed to get an eye to the crack in the trunk. And saw a most alarming sight!

Coming through the woods towards him was a couple of Neanderthal hunters. But they weren't carrying spears. They were carrying big stone axes and were talking in loud voices.

"No, green wood's no good for fires. It just fills your cave with smoke."

"Quite right. Dead wood's best. But where can you find a dead tree nowadays? They've all been cut down years ago."

"Yes, I can remember when I was a lad, you could . . . wait a minute! What's that?"

"It's a . . . a . . . dead tree."

"Where did it come from?"

"Don't be daft, they don't come from anywhere. They grow."

"But it wasn't here yesterday! And as far as I remember it's only mushrooms that grow in a night. Not trees. Especially dead ones."

"Perhaps it's magic!"

"Magic or no magic, it's good fire wood, and I'm going to cut it down."

The man stepped forward and swung his axe back.

"OH, NO YOU'RE NOT!" shouted a strange voice from the tree.

At that moment, Mum and Littlenose came out from amongst the trees and saw an incredible sight. In one direction a pair of brawny Neanderthal hunters were throwing away their axes, running for their lives, and screaming in terror. And, in the opposite direction a tree was running . . . also screaming in terror.

Mum and Littlenose ran as fast as they could. "It's all right, Dad," shouted Littlenose. "We won't let anyone cut you down."

But Dad was too terrified to listen. He burst out from the trees right in front of the caves, where the rest of the tribe were preparing to have lunch. A tree bewitched, they thought. A thousand times worse than even Littlenose and his spear. In a moment, every cooking fire had been abandoned and the tribe watched fearfully from their caves as Dad ran round and round.

Then, quite abruptly, Dad's strength gave out. As Mum and Littlenose came out of the forest they saw him come to a sudden stop, sway to and fro for a moment, then down he crashed in a great shower of rotten wood, bark, spiders, earwigs and creepy-crawlies as the tree trunk burst into a thousand pieces, and left Dad lying on the ground wondering if it were the end of the world.

The tribe looked on as Littlenose helped him to his feet. "Stupid game to play at

his age! You can see where that boy of his gets it all from," they said.

Mum fetched a pot of bear grease to rub on Dad's bruises. (Littlenose knew she'd use it for something.) And Littlenose didn't bother to ask if they were going to do more spear-throwing in the afternoon. He was already planning a super game to play with Two-Eyes after lunch.

Littlenose to the Rescue

Littlenose's people were really not very clever, and like a lot of people were suspicious of those who were. As far as they were concerned the Neanderthal way of doing things was the only right and proper way. Even people who *looked* different were thought slightly dangerous. And one person who was different was Uncle Redhead. He had flaming red hair and he could do things that most

Neanderthal men had never even heard of. Neanderthal folk were generally very dark. Nobody actually threatened Uncle Redhead or said anything impolite to his face, but there was a lot of talk among the tribe when he wasn't there. This made Littlenose very angry and he would shout, "You shouldn't say things like that about my Uncle Redhead. He's the cleverest person in the whole world!"

"There's such a thing as being too clever," he was told. The only other person who seemed to like Uncle Redhead was Mum. And he was her brother.

One day Uncle Redhead dropped in for a visit. "Just passing through," he said.

"Good," said Dad.

After supper, Littlenose went for a stroll before bedtime with Uncle Redhead. They walked along the river bank chatting about this and that, then sat on a rock by the water's edge and watched the ripples.

Uncle Redhead turned to Littlenose. "Tell me what you've been doing since I last saw you," he said. Littlenose mentioned a few things, then went on to describe his holiday with Uncle Juniper and his family in the mountains.

"I thought it would be dull," he said, "and it was to begin with. Then I had a narrow escape. I don't ever want to go back there again."

He described the evil creature which had left the huge footprints in the snow and had chased him over the mountainside. "Uncle Juniper's boys called it a Bigfoot." He had told no one else until now, and he half expected Uncle Redhead to laugh.

But his uncle nodded his head and said: "I've come across those creatures myself. They don't half smell." Littlenose nodded agreement. "The northern tribes have another name for them," went on Uncle Redhead. "Something like 'disgusting snowmen'. Very odd. Anyway, how did you escape?"

"The boys threw stones," said Littlenose. "I've never seen anyone throw stones as far or as hard as they did. I wish I could."

"As far as this?" said Uncle Redhead, tossing a pebble into the river.

"Much farther," said Littlenose.

"How about this, then," said Uncle Redhead. "Watch that log." And he pointed to a large piece of driftwood just visible on the far side of the river. Then he stepped behind Littlenose. Littlenose kept his eyes glued to the log. There was a sound behind him and a stone whirred over his head. Straining his eyes, Littlenose just made out the spurt in the water beside the log where the stone had landed.

Littlenose said nothing. He just stared open-mouthed and open-eyed in amazement. Nobody, not even Uncle Redhead could throw a stone as far as that! He turned to Uncle Redhead, who grinned. "Watch again, Littlenose," he said. "Watch that tall tree, where the herons nest." Littlenose again peered across the river to where the white shapes of the herons nests could just be seen standing guard over their ragged nests in the topmost branches. Again, there was a noise from Uncle Redhead and again a stone whizzed over Littlenose's head. But this time it was followed by the angry

squawk of enraged herons as the stone
zipped through the tree branches.

Uncle Redhead laughed and said,
"Wouldn't you like to be able to throw
stones like that?"

"Yes, *please*" said Littlenose.

Well, come here and I'll teach you," said
his uncle, at the same time holding up a
curious object. It was a leather pouch, with
two long rawhide thongs dangling from it.

Uncle Redhead took a pebble, placed it in the pouch, and whirled it round and round his head. Suddenly he let go of one of the thongs and next moment the pebble was flying across the river, so fast and far, it was almost out of sight.

"It's called a sling," said Uncle Redhead. "Some of the Straightnose tribes use them for hunting. *Our* people won't touch them. Too new-fangled for them, I suppose. But now it's your turn."

Littlenose held the sling carefully in his right hand as Uncle Redhead showed him, and placed a stone in the pouch. Then he swung it round his head. Faster and faster he whirled it until Uncle Redhead yelled, "Now! Let go!" And Littlenose *let* go. Completely. So that the sling as well as the stone landed in the water. Luckily,

 Littlenose
had not swung
it very hard, and
it was close enough
to the bank for
Uncle Redhead to
hook it out with a
long stick.

Next time,
Littlenose was
thinking so hard about not letting go
completely that he forgot to let go at all.
The thongs wound round and round his
head and the stone gave him a nasty bang
on the ear.

With his next attempt, he just missed
Uncle Redhead's eye, but it was a beginning.
By the time they returned to the cave
Littlenose could send a stone much farther

and harder than before, and more or less in
the direction he intended. Before he left,
Uncle Redhead said seriously: "A sling is
not a toy. It is a dangerous weapon. You
must only practise where there is no
chance of anyone being in the way. As a
hunter you should find it very useful."

As a junior hunter, Littlenose was
supposed to put in a lot of practice in
things like spear throwing and fire lighting
and tracking. Dad usually had to remind
him, but now, to his amazement,
Litttlenose spent all day and every day out
of doors practising. What Father didn't
know was that it was sling practice.
Littlenose didn't dare tell him. He had a
feeling that Dad wouldn't approve. As the
weeks went by, Littlenose became more
and more expert, until he could hit an oak

tree at a hundred paces.
He felt very pleased
with himself as he
made his way
home one
evening.
"You know,
Two-Eyes,"
he said to his
pet mammoth,

"I definitely think that I'm ready to take
my sling hunting. Tomorrow!"

Next morning, after breakfast, Littlenose
strolled out of the cave. He wasn't carrying
his spear, and Mum asked, "Where are you
going, dear? Aren't you practising?"

"Not today," he replied. "I'm just going
for a walk with Two-Eyes."

"Well, be good and don't be late," said

Mum. She didn't see the sling, tucked carefully out of sight inside Littlenose's furs.

They followed the trail by the river, then turned away to climb through the woods towards the high country where the best hunting was to be found. But they saw nothing. Littlenose thought this very strange, and even Two-Eyes began to look around, and sniff the air. He was acting very uneasily, and stopped more and more frequently to sniff the breeze and to spread his big ears to catch suspicious sounds. "Come on, Two-Eyes," said Littlenose. "There's nothing." But Two-Eyes' steps began to drag, and he went slower and slower until he stopped. He trumpeted softly and nudged Littlenose with his furry trunk. "It's too soon to go home," said Littlenose. "Tell you what. We'll have a rest among those trees over there."

The trees formed a small
wood, and Littlenose
found a comfortable grassy
bank where he lay down,
but Two-Eyes refused to
rest. He paced up and
down, sniffing and
listening, and growing more
agitated every moment.

At last Littlenose could
stand it no longer. He jumped
up. "For goodness' sake, Two-Eyes
. . ." Then, faintly, as if coming
from a long way off, he could
hear strange noises. It was a
confused mixture of animal
sounds and men's voices,
with bangings and rattlings

and the pounding of hooves.

Quickly, Littlenose climbed to the top of the tallest tree in the wood and peered across country. It was a moment before he saw anything, then he made out a long cloud of dust stretching across the horizon. "A stampede," thought Littlenose. "Probably bison. Well, this is the safest place to be." He called down to Two-Eyes. "Stay where you are. You'll be all right." But Two-Eyes was gone. Littlenose had a glimpse of him running as fast as his short hairy legs could carry him away from the approaching dust cloud.

The first warning that all was not well was the appearance of the stampeding animals. They were elk! At least two were. But there were half a dozen horses, and a woolly rhinoceros. Then some bison. Then several deer. More and more appeared, charging madly along, and all mixed up together. The noise of hooves was deafening as the huge crowd of galloping creatures thundered round and through the wood. They neighed, roared, whinnied, squealed and bellowed, and Littlenose wondered what made them run. Bison, he knew, stampeded often, and other animals might flee from something like a grass fire. But there was no sign of smoke. As the last small deer rushed under the tree and out again into the open, Littlenose saw the reason. A long line of men was advancing. They were rattling sticks and spears together, or beating on clay pots with skins stretched across the tops to make a loud booming. The men shouted and whooped as they drove the frightened animals before them. It was a hunting party.

A *Straightnose* hunting party!

Sometimes the Neanderthal folk used stampeding as a way of hunting, but not very successfully. More often than not the animals got the wrong idea, and it was the hunters who had to stampede to safety! But the Straightnoses were clever and highly organised. From high in the tree, Littlenose watched the line of men pass swiftly beneath him and on across the plain in the wake of their quarry. What they would do next, and how they would catch the animals, he didn't know. But somewhere out there was Two-Eyes, and he was sure as the elk and bison to be caught by the Straightnoses. Littlenose scrambled down and ran after the hunters as hard as he could.

By the time that Littlenose emerged into

the open, the line of Straightnose hunters
had passed out of sight. The trail was easy
to follow, and Littlenose panted along over
the trampled grass and deep hoof prints.
After a time, he became aware that the
noises in front were getting louder. They
seemed to come from a fold in the ground
which formed a broad hollow. Littlenose
crept toward the hollow and very
cautiously peered over the rim. He saw an
incredible sight. The hollow was packed
with animals. Elk, horses, rhinoceros and
deer milled about, bellowing and
squealing. The Straightnoses had set up
tall wooden stakes in the ground round the
edge of the hollow, and had tied long
branches between to make a rough fence.
One end was open, and the Straightnoses
were driving in the last animals with loud

yells and much waving of spears. As the last deer fled in panic into the trap, half a dozen brawny hunters lifted a long loose section of fence into place and fixed it fast with ropes. The Straightnoses turned to where a fire was burning some distance away and where they evidently intended to camp for the night.

Littlenose watched the trapped animals. They made plenty of noise, but didn't seem to be trying to escape. The fence looked quite flimsy, but even great beasts like the rhinoceros and elk were too frightened to realise it. But Littlenose was more interested in looking for one particular animal. It seemed unlikely that Two-Eyes had escaped, so he must be somewhere in there. In the dust it was hard to pick out something as small as a young mammoth,

and Littlenose was daring to hope that
Two-Eyes might have just got away when,
above the din, he heard a familiar squeaky
trumpeting. Directly below him, he saw a
small black shape pressed against the bars
of the trap, and a short trunk waving
forlornly through a gap. Somehow, he must
rescue Two-Eyes. But how? The Straightnoses
would spot him the moment that he
appeared in the hollow, and in any case,

he knew that he was too small to open the gate or make a gap for Two-Eyes to squeeze through. He didn't even have his spear. But he did have his sling. Tucked inside his furs so that he had forgotten all about it.

Quickly Littlenose picked up a stone, fitted it into the sling and sent it whizzing down into the hollow. It struck a rhinoceros on the ear. The rhino squealed, then jumped and butted a large elk with its horns. The elk lashed out with its hooves, missed the rhino, but caught a horse in the ribs. The horse went mad, snapping and biting at everything and, in a moment, there was uproar. The hunters came running and saw the animals in the trap fighting and struggling among themselves. They also saw that the fence was beginning to give way as the heavy creatures crashed

into it. Then one hunter shouted and
pointed. A whole section of stakes and
branches was sagging to the ground. The
Straightnoses began to run as again the
animals stampeded . . . with the
Straightnoses in front this time! Littlenose
screamed: "Up here, Two-Eyes!" And the
little mammoth heard his voice above the
din and scrambled out of the hollow to
join him.

Soon all the animals were gone. So were the Straightnoses and their camp. The trap was just a scattered mess of broken sticks.

Littlenose put his sling carefully back inside his furs. Then he took Two-Eyes' trunk in his hand, and together they set off for home, supper and bed.

The Music Stick

In Littlenose's day people ate fruit, fish and meat. Fruit they collected from the trees, fish they caught in the lakes and rivers, but for meat they had to go out and hunt. They hunted rabbits and birds, which was easy but not very rewarding, and they hunted woolly rhinoceros, elk and musk ox, which was much more rewarding but extremely dangerous. When hunting, the

Neanderthal man was likely to be hunted in turn by bears and sabre-toothed tigers. Most of the time they ate quite well. But occasionally for some inexplicable reason they would be unable to find anything to hunt, and had to make do with fish and fruit.

One day, Littlenose's dad returned from a brief hunting trip with other men of the tribe. His share of the bag was one small hare and two skinny pigeons. "Is that all?" cried

Mum in dismay. "It's hardly a mid-morning snack."

"It represents a week's stalking and chasing," said Dad. "And you had better make it last at least two meals, because I have no idea where the next lot's coming from."

Littlenose, of course, took the whole thing very badly. For one thing, instead of Dad going off and killing a deer which lasted the family for a whole week, Littlenose found himself wading about in cold water looking for fish which lasted for only one meal. Or else he was sent into the woods to dig for earth-nuts and pick mushrooms, which lasted only one course. As he returned to the cave with an aching back and sore fingers one morning, he saw Two-Eyes contentedly grazing on a clump of grass. "It's all right for you, Two-Eyes," he said. "You can get by on grass. What wouldn't I give for some meat. Roast rhinoceros, for instance. Or grilled elk."

"Or mammoth?" said a voice. It was one of the neighbours. He looked at Two-Eyes and licked his lips. "Just a thought," he said, and laughed. But the way he laughed turned Littlenose's blood cold. He hadn't thought about it before, but to a lot of people, Two-Eyes was obviously more a potential meal than a family pet. He wouldn't be at all surprised if Dad thought that way too. There and then Littlenose made up his mind. First thing next day he would take Two-Eyes and set off on a hunting trip of his own. For one thing, he was sure the grown-ups had been going about it in the wrong way, and for another Two-Eyes would be safer out of reach of peckish neighbours, not to mention his own family.

Next morning, Littlenose and Two-Eyes set off. They left the caves and climbed the hill towards the open plain. Then they set out confidently, examining the ground carefully for traces of game.

A butterfly flew to a clump of thistles

and flew off again. A swarm of ants hurried by, and a long, pink worm took cover in its burrow as a small brown bird hopped through the grass. Otherwise, Littlenose and Two-Eyes seemed to be the only living things of any size. Perhaps the grown-ups were right after all, and there was no game. Still, the day was early yet. They would press on and their luck was bound to change.

At noon, they stopped. Two-Eyes grazed, and Littlenose ate the rather squashed breakfast which had been tucked inside his furs. Then he lay down for a rest. The sun was warm, and he was almost asleep, when he sat up with a start. He had heard something. He reached for his spear, and saw that Two-Eyes was already alert, his big furry ears spread to catch the slightest sound. Then, it came again – a sort of muttering. Or was it? More of a grumbling, perhaps? It sounded like a whole herd of some sort of animal. Followed by Two-Eyes, Littlenose tip-toed in the direction of the sound, until it dawned on him that the sounds were men's *voices*! A great many men by the sound of things, and all talking at once. But that didn't make things any safer!

Littlenose was right to be careful. It was a crowd of Straightnoses – a hunting party. And a successful one at that. The men were laden down with game, and off to one side some were cutting up the fresh meat while others were lighting a fire. They were obviously going to have a feast to celebrate their success. And Littlenose realised that the Straightnoses had driven off all the game and caught it themselves, leaving none for the Neanderthal folk. And if that wasn't bad enough, Littlenose now had to crouch, hidden in the rocks, and watch as the Straightnose cooks roasted the meat. The meat sizzled and the gravy dripped, and Littlenose tried to stop his mouth from watering at the marvellous smell, which he had almost forgotten. "But," he thought, "the Straightnoses will be moving on soon, and they're sure to have left some scraps behind. I might even find enough to take home to Mum and Dad. And won't they be pleased with me!"

At last, the Straightnoses appeared to have eaten enough. They sat back, picking their teeth and patted their stomachs contentedly. They cleared a space in the centre of the hollow, then began to sing. Two of them ran into the centre and began to dance. It was a hunter's victory dance,

and the singing grew louder and the clapping
faster as the dancers leapt and whirled.

Despite his hunger Littlenose found
himself tapping his feet in time. He leaned
out from the rocks, but no one noticed
him, and it was getting late and the
darkness was falling. The only light came

from the fire, and the rosy glow helped to make a very festive scene. Littlenose had forgotten that he was hungry. He was caught up in the rhythm of the music, and as he listened he realised that there was more than singing and clapping.

There was another sound! Littlenose couldn't make out what it was, but it was part of the music, and the singing and clapping were keeping time to it. He listened, and found himself not only tapping his feet but snapping his fingers to the exciting rhythm. The singing and clapping paused for a moment, and now Littlenose could hear more clearly a steady RATTLE! RATTLE! RATTLE! with a JINGLE! JINGLE! JINGLE! on top. What or who was making this exciting music he couldn't see, but he leaned out from his hiding place to hear better. Luckily the Straightnoses were enjoying their party so much that no one spotted him. Littlenose had had a long day and started to nod. So he made his way back to where Two-Eyes had already curled up into a black woolly ball for the night, and snuggled down beside him.

It was the cold that woke Littlenose. The grass and Two-Eyes' fur were covered with dew, and the sun was just coming over the sky-line. Littlenose was not only cold, he was ravenous. He stretched, then made his way carefully back to the edge of the hollow.

The hollow was empty. There was not a Straightnose in sight. But the remains of their cooking fire still smouldered, and Littlenose remembered how hungry he was, and hoped that there might be scraps of food left. He was lucky. Almost immediately he found a bone with lots of meat still on it, and throwing some twigs on to the embers of the fire, he sat down to breakfast.

"Now," he thought. "I must find some meat to take home. If I find enough, perhaps they won't be so mad at me for staying out all night." He searched, but there was nothing to be found except bare bones – the Straightnoses had either eaten or carried away everything else. Littlenose had decided that he might just as well give up and head for home, when he glimpsed something in the long grass. Another bone, perhaps. Maybe with meat on it. Littlenose took a closer look. But it wasn't a bone. It had evidently been left behind by the Straightnoses, because it was carved and polished. It was a pole, like a spear handle, but it didn't have a point like a spear.

Instead, two bison horns were fixed to the end, with a decoration of a wilting wreath of flowers. Magic? It was a well-known fact that the Straightnoses were adept at magic, particularly in hunting. Littlenose walked all around the horned pole, ready to run at the first sign of danger. But it just lay there in the damp grass. Taking a deep breath, Littlenose bent down and carefully took hold of the pole, holding it at arm's length. He moved it closer for a better look . . . and dropped it in terror! It had given out a rattling noise. After several long moments, and shaking all over, he tried again. This time it not only rattled but jingled as well. Holding his breath, he deliberately shook the pole. It rattled and jingled as before. The faster and harder he shook, the louder and faster came the sound:

JINGLE! JINGLE! RAT-TAT-TAT!
JINGLE! JINGLE! RAT-TAT-TAT!

It was the music to which the Straightnoses
had been dancing the night before! Now
Littlenose began to dance. Up and down
and to and fro, skipping round the fire, and
all the time shaking the stick in time with

his steps. He danced until he was breathless, then dropped down on the grass to rest. He examined his new toy. There were stones or seeds or something in the bison horns, which made the rattling, while several large sea-shells strung below jingled together. The flowers were only for decoration. But it was time he went home. He called to Two-Eyes, and set off, dancing to the sound of the music stick.

Now, while Littlenose had been worrying about being in trouble for staying out all night, the truth is that no one had missed him. Something much more exciting was happening back at the caves. Just after Littlenose had set off on his hunting trip, Nosey the tracker had rushed into the middle of the caves shouting: "I've found it! I've found it!"

"Found what?" everyone called.

"MEAT! Enough for everybody!" cried Nosey.

"Where?" they asked.

"In the forest," said Nosey.

"Elk? Rhinoceros? Deer?"

"Cattle," said Nosey, and everyone took a step back before they all started shouting at once.

The forest cattle were greatly feared by the Neanderthal folk. Sabre-toothed tigers and bears attacked people to eat them, which seemed reasonable in a land where food was hard to come by at the best of times. But the forest cattle ate grass, and attacked people for the fun of it, or so it appeared. They were also very large, very cunning, and extremely fierce. But this was a solitary bull which Nosey had tracked to

an oak thicket near the edge of the forest. No one had ever hunted a forest bull before. The hunters usually took particular care to avoid them.

"It'll be easy," Nosey said. "We'll flush it out. One party of hunters will go around from the rear, making all the noise they can, and the rest will be waiting at the front to catch the bull as the noise frightens it and it rushes out."

It took the rest of the day to get organised, particularly forming the two parties. No one was sure whether it was safer going *into* a thicket containing a dangerous animal, or waiting for it to come charging *out*. At last it was agreed that first thing after breakfast next day they would set out.

The hunters left in high spirits, which were quickly dampened when they discovered that catching a forest bull was not as easy as Nosey supposed. He had reckoned without the bull itself, which was old and very cunning. It had been hunted so many times that it knew more about hunting than the hunters.

They formed their line on the far side of the oak thicket and started pushing through the undergrowth, shouting, clapping their hands and rattling spears together. The great white bull lay in the thickest part and listened to the racket. It was safe where it was, because the hunters were quite unable to force their way through. The bull had heard shouting and clapping so often that it no longer bothered him.

But the hunters were bothered. The beaters emerged from their thicket . . . but no bull. They stood arguing and shouting. Then they stopped and looked back. There was rushing and a crashing, as out rushed the bull, its eyes wide with terror. It was so frightened that it didn't even see the hunters. Recovering from their surprise, they were on the bull in an instant, and soon it lay dead on the grass.

But what had made the bull rush out like that? Something must have frightened it. Then a hunter put his hand to his ear and said "Listen!" And through the trees they heard a sound. They had never heard anything like it before. It was weird. Frightening. Eyes wide like the bull's had been, they stood rooted to the spot as it came nearer:

JINGLE! JINGLE! RAT-TAT-TAT!
JINGLE! JINGLE! RAT-TAT-TAT!

Something was moving in the bushes. The hunters turned to flee . . . and Littlenose came dancing out of the forest, shaking the music stick in rhythm as he came. He hadn't even seen or heard the bull, he was so engrossed in his music. He couldn't understand what all the fuss was about. And what a fuss! The hunters yelled and

shouted about giving people frights,
picking up strange objects and that sort of
thing. But, when someone pointed out that
without Littlenose they would not have
caught the bull, they calmed down.

That night the tribe held a great dance

to celebrate the successful hunt, and when the hunters danced their victory dance Littlenose was in the place of honour, making the music on his music stick.

100,000 YEARS AGO people wore no clothes. They lived in caves and hunted animals for food. They were called NEANDERTHAL.

50,000 YEARS AGO when Littlenose lived, clothes were made out of fur. But now there were other people. Littlenose called them Straightnoses. Their proper name is HOMO SAPIENS.

5,000 YEARS AGO there were no Neanderthal people left. People wore cloth as well as fur. They built in wood and stone. They grew crops and kept cattle.

1,000 YEARS AGO towns were built, and men began to travel far from home by land and sea to explore the world.

500 YEARS AGO towns became larger, as did the ships in which men travelled. The houses they built were very like those we see today.

100 YEARS AGO people used machines to do a lot of the harder work. They could now travel by steam train. Towns and cities became very big, with factories as well as houses.

TODAY we don't hunt for our food, but buy it in shops. We travel by car and aeroplane. Littlenose would not understand any of this. Would YOU like to live as Littlenose did?